SABAN'S POWER RANGERS LOST GALAXY

STRANGE NEW WORLD

A novelization by Eliza Willard

Based on the teleplays by Judd Lynn

A PARACHUTE PRESS BOOK

A PARACHUTE PRESS BOOK
Parachute Publishing, L.L.C.
156 Fifth Avenue
New York, New York 10010

Printed in the U.S.A.
October 1999
ISBN: 1-57351-001-7
10 9 8 7 6 5 4 3 2 1

Prologue

The battle between good and evil begins again!

The universe has been at peace—thanks to the Power Rangers.

But during the peaceful years, Earth has become very crowded. So the people of Earth have built a new space colony called *Terra Venture*. *Terra Venture* is a huge space colony run by the Galactic Space Alliance. It will travel through space, searching for new frontiers—new planets where humans can safely live.

Now an evil king named Scorpius threatens *Terra Venture*. He wants to rule the universe! And he is so powerful, no one can stop him!

But five teenagers are willing to try. Maya, Kai, Kendrix, Leo, and Damon will need all the power they can get to stop Scorpius. They'll need the strength of Power Rangers!

1

"Did I miss anything?" Maya asked. She strained to see what was happening in the village square.

"No," the girl next to her whispered. "No one has been chosen yet."

Maya nodded. She swung herself up into a tree hoping she would see better.

Maya and her people lived on the peaceful jungle planet of Mirinoi. It looked like many places on Earth—but it was not Earth. It wasn't even in the same galaxy as Earth. Mirinoi was far, far away, in another part of the universe.

Maya was eighteen years old. She had long brown hair and fiery dark eyes. She wore loose, tattered clothes, like all the others in the village.

Everyone on Mirinoi had gathered for an important ceremony. Jera, the leader of the tribe, stood in front of a huge rock. Five golden swords were thrust deep into the rock. Only their handles stuck out.

"These five Quasar Sabers were

the weapons of the mighty Power Rangers. They were placed in this rock three thousand years ago," Jera said. "No one can free the sabers until they prove themselves worthy. The worthy ones will harness the mighty powers of the Quasar Sabers." He raised both hands. "Who will free a saber? Who will become our new champion?"

One by one, the strongest warriors of Mirinoi tried to pull the sabers out. And one by one, they failed.

Maya bit her lip. *Is there no one who can protect us?* she thought.

Her people needed help desperately. The evil king Scorpius had sent Stingwinger troops armed with blasters to take over Mirinoi. The villagers had no weapons. They had no way to defend themselves.

Were they doomed?

Suddenly Maya heard a rustle of leaves in the jungle. She peered through the thick palm trees.

Stingwingers!

The ugly, buglike creatures buzzed into the village square. They looked like man-sized hornets, with shimmering wings and disgusting insect heads. But they had normal, human-like arms and legs.

Their huge captain, Furio, strode to the center of the square. Maya shuddered at the sight of his evil, twisted face.

"Stingwingers, attack!" he cried.

The villagers screamed as the Stingwingers came after them. The creatures kicked, punched, and stung people with their stingers. Hidden up in the tree, Maya watched with horror.

"The Quasar Sabers!" Furio roared. "I must have them!" He reached for one of the swords and yanked on the handle.

It didn't move.

"You'll never be worthy!" Maya shouted. She swung down from the tree on a vine.

"After her!" Furio screeched.

Maya raced through the jungle—with a crowd of Stingwingers following right behind her!

2

"I can't believe it!" Kendrix Morgan checked her watch. "Only six more hours!"

Kendrix stood in the *Terra Venture* command center with her friends Mike Corbett and Kai Chen. All three wore battle fatigues.

Terra Venture, an enormous space colony, was orbiting Earth.

The space colony was a spaceship as big as a city, where people could live. In six hours it would blast off to find new worlds in new galaxies.

Kendrix, Mike, and Kai were officers on *Terra Venture*. They watched as shuttles brought hundreds of excited people from Earth to the space colony.

Kendrix straightened her glasses. Her blond hair was pulled back neatly in a ponytail, as always. She worked as a scientist on *Terra Venture*.

Kai, like Kendrix, was neat and under control. His dark hair was cut short. His uniform was in perfect order.

Mike was an important aide to

the commander of *Terra Venture*. He had brown hair and a strong face. He made sure people got their jobs done—and done right.

"Prepare for a training exercise on the moon," Mike told Kendrix and Kai. "It's probably our last chance to practice—before we face a *real* battle!"

No one knew what kind of creatures they would face in outer space. The Galactic Space Alliance wanted its soldiers to be prepared for anything.

Kai and Kendrix marched toward the heliship that would take them to the moon.

Meanwhile, on Earth, a young

man named Leo watched the *Terra Venture* shuttles take off. He was slim and wiry, with messy brown hair. He wore a red shirt and jeans.

"If only I could go on *Terra Venture!*" he said, pacing in front of his viewscreen. But he didn't have a passport. Everyone wanted to go to Terra Venture, but only a few were given the special papers they needed to board the space colony. The guards would not let anyone on the shuttles without a passport.

I'll show them, Leo thought. He had an idea. He would sneak on board *Terra Venture*.

Leo sneaked into the cargo area. Workers loaded crates of supplies onto the shuttle.

Leo leaped onto a luggage cart. It zipped toward the cargo hold of the shuttle.

But then a guard spotted him. "Hey—you!" the guard yelled. "Stop!"

Leo jumped off the luggage cart and darted behind a crate. Two guards chased him. Leo dodged them and hitched a ride on a moving forklift.

The guards looked around. "Where did he go?" one asked.

The other spoke into his radio. "Attention! We had a stowaway, but we lost him. Everyone keep your eyes open."

Leo laughed to himself. The forklift stopped at the cargo hold of the shuttle. Leo sneaked aboard. A worker slammed the door shut.

The shuttle took off for *Terra Venture*.

Ha! Leo thought happily. *I'm going into outer space! No one can stop me now!*

3

The shuttle landed on Terra Venture. Leo sneaked out of the hold. He slipped away from the shuttle port and gazed at the space colony.

"Wow," he sighed.

Terra Venture was huge, sparkling, and buzzing with activity. Tall skyscrapers gleamed above him. Electric cars hummed down the brand-new streets. People hurried about wearing brightly colored uniforms.

"Hey—you! Stop right there!"

Leo whirled around. Two guards had spotted him!

He dashed up an escalator. The guards chased after him.

Leo hurried down a hallway, glancing over his shoulder. He raced around a corner and—*boom!*—knocked over a girl.

"I'm so sorry!" Leo said.

A young man stood beside the girl. They were Kai and Kendrix. Kai scowled at Leo.

Leo helped Kendrix to her feet. He thought he had never seen such a pretty girl before.

"You ought to be more careful," Kai scolded. "Come on, Kendrix. We've got to hurry. The heliship leaves for the moon in five minutes!"

Kendrix glanced back at Leo as Kai hustled her away.

Suddenly, two guards ran down the hall. Leo darted through a door. The guards didn't notice him.

"Did you see a guy run by here?" the guards asked Kai and Kendrix. "Slim, short dark hair, wearing a red shirt? He's a stowaway."

Kai opened his mouth to speak, but Kendrix stopped him. She guessed that they were talking about Leo.

"I'm sorry, but I don't think

we've seen him," she lied.

The guards hurried away. Kai stared at Kendrix, speechless.

Leo slipped out the door and ran down another hallway. He passed a rack of battle fatigues.

He skidded to a stop. *Battle fatigues! That's perfect!* he thought. He grabbed some clothes and ducked around a corner. A few minutes later he walked down the hallway—dressed like a soldier.

Lines of soldiers marched past him. Leo joined them. *I wonder where we're going,* he thought, excited.

He followed the soldiers onto a jet heliship. The commander passed out laser weapons.

"These are the very last defense exercises we'll have before *Terra Venture* leaves," the commander said. "Watch for your enemy. Stay calm. And remember—never, ever leave a team member behind."

Leo glanced at the other soldiers packed into the heliship. Toward the front he spotted Kai and Kendrix.

Oh, no, Leo thought. He pulled his cap down low over his face. *I hope they won't give me away.*

But they didn't seem to notice him. After a while, Leo began to relax.

Soon the heliship landed on the moon. The soldiers poured out. At once, lasers began to blast them.

Leo ducked behind a rock.

Help! he thought. *What did I get myself into?*

Kai led a group of soldiers, including Kendrix, across the rough surface of the moon. Leo followed them, dodging the laser blasts.

The group paused under a sharp cliff. Suddenly, a laser blasted into the cliff. The ground shuddered.

Leo glanced up. Huge chunks of rock broke loose from the top of the cliff.

The rocks were about to crash— right on top of Kendrix!

Leo gasped. He bolted over to Kendrix and pushed her aside—just in time! The huge rocks thundered past them.

Leo and Kendrix lifted their heads as the dust cleared.

"Thanks," Kendrix said. Then she recognized Leo. "It's you!"

Kai noticed Leo, too. He hurried over and grabbed him.

"You're the stowaway!" Kai cried.

Then Mike ran over to them. "Is everybody okay?" he asked.

When Mike saw Leo, his jaw dropped. "Leo! What are you doing here?"

"Well, I …" Leo stammered.

"You know him?" Kendrix asked.

"He's my little brother," Mike said.

Kai and Kendrix stared at Leo.

"I told you not to come to *Terra*

Venture," Mike barked at Leo. "It's dangerous. Anything could happen. The colony might never go back to Earth—ever!"

Leo pushed his brother away. "I want to see what's out in space as badly as you do," he declared.

Mike stared at his little brother. He knew there was nothing he could do. If he sent Leo back to Earth, Leo would just find another way to get aboard *Terra Venture*.

At last Mike slapped Leo on the back. "Let's go!" he ordered. "Come on, troops! This is an important training exercise!"

Leo grinned. He knew what that meant.

Mike was going to let him stay!

4

On the distant planet Mirinoi, Maya frantically raced through the jungle. Dozens of buzzing Stingwingers chased her.

Maya leaped through the trees. She swung from vine to vine. She was too quick for the Stingwingers.

But the Stingwingers began to shoot at her with their blasters.

One sent a fireball hurtling after her.

Maya dodged the fireball. It exploded in front of her.

Maya couldn't stop. She kept running—right through the flaming explosion!

That very moment, on the moon, something strange happened. Leo heard a loud crack of thunder. In front of him, the air shimmered.

"Whoa!" he cried, jumping back.

A round, glowing hole opened up in the cliff.

"A dimensional portal!" Mike gasped.

Suddenly, a dark haired girl flew out of the hole. She tumbled right into Mike and Kai. It was Maya!

Five Stingwingers burst through the hole after her. All five of them immediately began to attack!

Mike, Kai, Kendrix, and Leo could see that Maya was in trouble. They blasted the Stingwingers with their lasers.

The Stingwingers shot back. One of them grabbed Maya. Mike kicked the Stingwinger off her.

Maya whirled and slammed her foot into another Stingwinger. It flew backwards and crunched against a rock.

At last, beaten, the Stingwingers retreated through the dimensional portal. Back to the planet Mirinoi.

The five teens stared after them.

"What just happened?" Mike asked Maya. "Who are you?"

"My name is Maya," she explained. "My home is the planet Mirinoi—or what's left of it."

"I've never heard of Mirinoi," Kendrix said.

Maya stepped up to the glowing hole in the cliff. "I've got to get back," she said. "Scorpius will destroy my world if he gets the Quasar Sabers!"

"If who gets what?" Kai asked. He looked confused.

Kendrix grabbed Maya's arm. "Wait! You could get hurt!"

Leo stepped forward. "Come on, let's go with her!"

"Are you nuts?" Kai protested.

"We have no idea what's in there!"

"It doesn't matter," Leo said. "She needs our help."

Kendrix joined Leo and Maya. "I'm going, too."

"Mike, we can't go," Kai said. "*Terra Venture* is leaving in a few hours. It won't wait for anyone!"

Mike stared at Maya's troubled face. He knew he had to help her.

"Stay here. We'll be back soon," he promised Kai. "Take my little brother with you."

"No!" Leo protested. "I'm going with you!"

"No, you're not," Mike declared. He turned to Maya and Kendrix. "Are you ready?"

The girls nodded. Maya,

Kendrix, and Mike ran through the shimmering portal and disappeared.

Leo watched them, speechless. Then he ran toward the portal. It was beginning to fade.

"Leo! Don't!" Kai shouted.

Leo leaped through the hole. Then, in a flash of light, he completely disappeared.

5

Kai stared at the portal as it faded to nothing. The hole in the cliff had closed. The portal was gone.

What should I do? Kai wondered.

Groups of soldiers hurried past him. "Come on!" one soldier called to Kai. "The transports are leaving any minute!"

Kai kept watching the cliff, hoping the portal would open again. But it didn't. There was no way to follow Leo.

Finally, Kai returned to the heliship and sat quietly. He remembered what the commander had said before the exercise.

"*Never, ever leave a team member behind.*"

"I shouldn't have left them," Kai said to himself. "I should have gone with my friends."

As the heliship landed on *Terra Venture*, something caught Kai's eye. A scrap of yellow paper on the floor.

Kai picked up the paper. It was a flier. "Visit the *Astro Megaship* Museum," the flier said.

An idea struck Kai like the blast of a laser. "That's it!" he cried.

He hurried through *Terra Venture* to the shuttle port. He jumped onto a shuttle back to Earth. He raced to the *Astro Megaship* Museum.

The *Astro Megaship* was the spaceship used by the famous Power Rangers, back when they were battling to save the universe from evil. The ship sat in a large white building in the middle of the city. Tourists lined up to see the ship and buy souvenirs. Alpha 5, a robot who had worked with the famous Power Rangers, acted as a tour guide.

Kai needed to get the tourists

"No one can free the sabers until they prove themselves worthy," Jera tells the mighty warriors of Mirinoi.

Furio's Stingwinger army waits in the jungle, ready to attack.

Maya races through the jungle with the Stingwingers hot on her trail!

"Tell me how to free the Quasar Sabers!" demands
Furio. "Or I'll destroy your whole planet!"

Kai slams a Stingwinger with a spinning kick!

The five teenagers learn the secret of the Quasar Sabers and morph into Power Rangers!

out of the ship if his plan was going to work. He pushed through the crowds. "Exit the museum, please," he said to them. "Everyone, please leave calmly."

Alpha 5 tapped Kai on the back. "Excuse me," he asked. "What's going on?"

"Um—" Kai had to think of something to say, fast. "The ship is being recommissioned. For a special top-secret assignment."

"Top-secret assignment?" Alpha said. "You mean—?"

"That's right," Kai said. "She's going to fly again."

"Fly?" Kai heard a voice speak behind him. "This is some kind of joke, right?"

Kai whirled around to see a handsome young man standing behind him. He wore greasy overalls and carried a wrench.

"Who are you?" Kai demanded.

"Damon Henderson," the young man replied. "I'm the mechanic around here. I know this ship inside and out. So believe me when I say this is a museum, not a spaceship."

"No one told *me* about any secret mission!" Alpha put in.

"Yeah," Damon said suspiciously. "If you're on a GSA mission, let's see your orders."

Alpha and Damon looked Kai in the eye. Kai knew it was time to tell the truth.

"Okay," he admitted. "I don't

have any orders. It's a long story, but my friends went through a dimensional portal to save another world. The portal closed. The *Astro Megaship* is the only craft that has a chance of getting through. And if I can't save them, they're gone. Forever!"

Alpha and Damon glanced at each other. This was serious.

"I'll need your help," Kai said to Damon. "You said you know the ship inside and out. I don't."

"I wish I could help your friends," Damon said. "But you'll be lucky if this thing even gets off the ground."

"Fine," Kai snapped. "Then leave if you're going to. I'll fly the ship by myself." He prepared to start the ship. "Alpha, how do we start the engines?"

"Ay, yi, yi," Alpha sighed.

Kai and Alpha pressed some buttons. The engines began to roar. The ship rattled and shook. The lights flickered off and on.

"Ay, yi, yi!" Alpha cried. "We'll never make it!"

Damon shook his head. "This is crazy," he muttered to himself. Then he pushed Kai aside. "Sit down," he said. "And watch how a pro does it."

Damon started flipping lots of switches. The lights stopped flickering. The engines hummed as the ship began to lift off. Up, up, up!

Kai held his breath as the ship crashed through the roof of the museum. Damon hit another button. Full power! The engines roared as the megaship zoomed away from Earth and into space.

A few moments later, Kai spotted a shimmering portal hanging in space.

"That's it!" he cried. "That looks just like the portal my friends went through."

"All right," said Damon. "We'll try to bust through. Buckle your seat belts!"

Damon grabbed the controls and pulled as hard as he could.

The ship flew toward the portal, faster, faster. . . .

Whoosh! The Astro Megaship blasted through the portal.

"We made it!" Damon cried.

Kai and Damon stared at the viewing screen. Multicolored stars and asteroids zipped past them— blue, green, pink, purple.

The three travellers found themselves in a strange new galaxy!

6

"We must be very quiet," Maya warned. She tiptoed through the jungle of Mirinoi. Mike, Kendrix, and Leo followed. "Stingwingers are everywhere."

Just then they heard a low hum. Maya signaled for everyone to duck. They hid in the tall grass.

Three Stingwingers buzzed past.

"Ugh," Kendrix muttered.

The teens rose again. Maya scanned the jungle. All clear for now. They moved on.

At last, they reached the village square. Maya and the others hid in the trees and watched.

Two Stingwingers held Jera, the wise man, near the Quasar Sabers. Furio, the Stingwinger leader, stood over Jera.

"Tell me how to free the Quasar Sabers!" Furio demanded. "Or I'll destroy your whole planet!"

"You'll never release them," Jera insisted. "You weren't chosen!"

"I'm getting tired of you, old man," Furio grumbled. He stepped toward Jera and raised his sword.

Maya gasped. She leaped out from the trees.

"Don't touch him!" she shouted.

Furio stopped and turned toward Maya. "Says who?" he asked with a snicker.

Leo jumped to Maya's side. Kendrix and Mike rushed to join them.

"All of us, that's who!" Leo cried.

Furio laughed. "Just the four of you?"

"Wrong. The *six* of us!" Kai declared.

Kai and Damon had arrived! The others gasped with surprise.

Furio began to laugh, a cold and evil laugh. "Stingwingers!" he screeched. "Destroy them!"

The Stingwingers attacked! Two of them grabbed Leo. Mike and Kendrix kicked them away.

Maya swung from a vine, knocking three Stingwingers to the ground. Damon and Kai furiously whirled around as the Stingwingers kept coming, one after another.

Furio raised his mighty sword against Mike. Mike grabbed a stick to defend himself. But Furio whacked the stick away with his sword.

Mike stumbled and lost his balance. He fell against the large rock.

Furio raised his sword again. He prepared to strike.

Desperate, Mike reached behind him. His hand clutched something metal. Mike grabbed it without thinking.

Shing! Out of the rock slid a Quasar Saber!

Furio swung his sword. Mike blocked it with the saber.

The saber crackled with bolts of electricity. Mike stared at it, amazed.

"The Quasar Saber!" Furio yelled. "Give it to me!"

Mike called to his friends. "Guys! Over here!"

The others hurried to the rock. Kendrix reached for a saber and pulled it smoothly from the rock. Then Kai and Damon each pulled out a saber.

Maya wrapped her fingers around the last saber. She tugged

on the saber. It slid easily from the rock.

The sabers gleamed in the five teens' hands. Leo watched them, amazed.

A feeling of strength and power sizzled through their bodies.

"We've been chosen!" Maya cried. "We've been chosen!"

7

"No!" Furio shouted. "No one but I can have the Quasar Sabers!"

He raised his sword to the sky. Glowing orange energy whirled around the tip, growing stronger and brighter.

Then Furio struck his sword into the ground. The evil orange energy spread quickly across the land.

Everything it touched turned to stone! Houses, trees—even people!

"Look out!" Kai shouted. The evil energy was moving toward them!

"We've got to get out of here!" Mike cried.

Clutching their sabers, the teens turned and ran through the thick jungle. The orange energy rippled after them. Behind them, everything turned to stone.

"You won't escape me!" Furio bellowed.

He struck the ground with his mighty sword. The ground cracked apart. A huge hole opened up before him.

Then Furio fired a laser blast at the teens. It jolted them off their feet and sent them flying.

"Whoa!" Mike tumbled across the ground—and fell into the deep hole!

"Mike!" Leo shouted. He hurried to the edge of the hole and looked down.

Mike clung to the side, barely holding on.

"Give me your hand!" Leo called. He reached down for Mike. Mike hung just out of reach. He tried to stretch a hand up toward Leo.

Mike's foot slipped. Rocks crumbled under his grip. He slid a little farther down.

"I can't hold on!" he said.

"Please Mike, give me your hand," Leo insisted.

Mike slipped down even farther. Leo stretched down as far as he could. He nearly fell into the hole!

"Leo," Mike said. "Take the saber."

"No," Leo said. "I can't. Give me your hand!" He didn't care about the saber. He wanted to save his brother!

"Leo, you have to!" Mike told him. Rocks crumbled under his feet. He was barely hanging on. "Hurry!"

Leo reached down as far as he could and grabbed the saber.

"You carry on for me," Mike said. "You can do it."

"Mike...no..." Leo's eyes grew misty with tears.

"I've always been proud of you," Mike said. "And I always will be."

With that, Mike slipped and fell down, down, down into the hole.

"*Noooooo!*" Leo screamed.

The hole closed over Mike.

8

**Leo and the others stared at the
ground in shock.**

Then Leo leaped to his feet and
raised the saber. Angrily, he whirled
around to face Furio.

Furio laughed. Leo charged at
him.

Furio knocked Leo away with his
sword. Leo fell to the ground.

The others hurried to help Leo to his feet. Leo raised his saber, ready to attack Furio again.

But suddenly, the saber began to glow. Leo pointed it to the sky as it shimmered bright gold.

One by one, the other sabers began to glow, too. Kendrix touched the tip of her saber to Leo's. Then Kai joined in, then Damon. When Maya raised her saber and touched it to the other four, a brilliant golden light flashed.

Furio shielded his eyes from the light.

Then an amazing thing happened. Leo, Kendrix, Kai, Damon, and Maya morphed into the Power Rangers!

Leo turned into the Red Ranger, the Lion!

Kendrix morphed into the Pink Ranger, the Wildcat!

Kai became the Blue Ranger, the Gorilla!

Damon became the Green Ranger, the Condor!

Maya turned into the Yellow Ranger, the Wolf!

The five teenagers stared at themselves. They couldn't believe it! They were Power Rangers!

Leo the Red Ranger felt an awesome power surge through his body. He aimed his saber at Furio.

Furio fired his laser at the Red Ranger. The Red Ranger ran right through the laser fire. He struck at

Furio with his saber.

But Furio fought back. Meanwhile, the evil Stingwingers attacked the other Power Rangers.

"Look out!" Damon, the Green Ranger, called. He pointed.

The evil orange energy! It was spreading toward them!

"Run!" cried Kai, the Blue Ranger.

The Power Rangers ran for their lives through the jungle. The Stingwingers took off after them.

Kendrix, the Pink Ranger, pointed up ahead. "The *Astro Megaship*!" she shouted.

They rushed onto the ship. Leo, the Red Ranger, paused for a moment at the entrance.

"I can't leave Mike back there!" he said.

"You can't stay!" cried the Blue Ranger. He pulled the Red Ranger inside the ship. The ramp closed behind them.

The five Power Rangers hurried to the bridge.

"Alpha, start the ship!" the Blue Ranger ordered.

"Ay, yi, yi!" Alpha cried. "Power Rangers!" He couldn't believe his eyes. "What in the world happened?"

The Power Rangers pulled off their helmets. "We'll explain later, Alpha," Kai said. "Right now we've got to get out of here!"

Alpha grabbed the controls.

"Everybody hold on!" he shouted.

The ship jolted and lifted off the ground. Beneath it, the last bit of green on Mirinoi turned to stone.

Furio angrily watched the *Astro Megaship* take off.

On the megaship, Leo stared at the viewing screen. Maya came up and stood beside him. The planet Mirinoi faded into the distance.

"Goodbye, my home," Maya said softly.

"Goodbye, Mike," Leo whispered.

"All right, Alpha," Kai said. "Take us back through the dimensional portal."

Alpha checked a computer reading. "Ay, yi, yi!" he cried in alarm.

"The portal is closing! We're not going to make it through!"

Damon grabbed the controls. "Divert all power to the shields," he ordered. "Hyper-accelerators to Level Five." He turned to the other Rangers. "Do we feel lucky?" he asked.

No one answered.

"Bad question," Damon said. "Hold on!"

He pulled on the controls. The ship raced toward the portal. Damon fired the megalasers. They blasted the portal, just barely keeping it open.

Whoosh! The ship slammed through the portal. Lights flashed. The Power Rangers held on tight as the ship shook.

A second later, everything was calm.

Damon glanced at the viewing screen. They were back in their own galaxy.

"We made it!" he said.

The other Rangers cheered. All except Maya. She was staring in awe at her new Power Ranger uniform.

"Do you know what this means?" she said quietly.

The other Rangers gathered around to listen.

"Those swords," Maya said. "The Quasar Sabers. They were put in that rock three thousand years ago. Every warrior in the galaxy tried to free them. But none could."

Maya's friends listened carefully to her story.

"Until now," Maya went on. "Don't you see? We have all been chosen—to fight evil. To be the new Power Rangers!"

9

The small fading dimensional portal rippled in space. With a blinding flash, the *Scorpion Stinger* blasted through it.

Inside the *Scorpion Stinger*, Furio stepped out of the shadows. He marched through the dark ship toward his leader, Scorpius.

Scorpius was the most horrible

villain of all time. His monstrous body, slick with ooze, grew out of a pedestal in the middle of his throne room.

Furio bowed before Scorpius. "We've passed through the portal," he announced.

"At last. Now get me the Quasar Sabers!" Scorpius commanded. "And destroy those who took them! All of them!"

Meanwhile, Terra Venture was getting ready to begin its mission. The space colony was crowded with cheering people.

Kai and Kendrix, dressed in their GSA uniforms, slipped out of an elevator into the command center.

"I can't believe it," Kendrix whispered. "Terra Venture is about to blast off!"

"Yeah," Kai agreed. "We made it back here just in time!"

The countdown began. The commander stepped up to the controls. "Fire thrusters!" he ordered. "Take us out of orbit." Then he faced the crowd with a smile. "Let's go find a new world."

And Terra Venture sped away from Earth.

Kai and Kendrix watched the viewing screen with excitement. They still couldn't believe that they and their new friends were Power Rangers!

"I have a feeling our powers are

going to be put to the test," Kai told Kendrix.

"Yeah," Kendrix agreed. "But I think it's going to be a really great adventure!"